When The Pacific Ocean Cam

Tsunami in Crescent City
California
March 27, 1964.

The True Story of the Gee Family

By Beverly J Raffaele

"When the Pacific Ocean
Came Through Our Front Door"

When The Pacific Ocean Came Through Our Front Door

Beverly J Raffaele

ISBN: 978-0-557-04411-5

A Personal Account
of the Good Friday Tidal Wave
March 27, 1964

A True Story

"When the Pacific Ocean
Came Through
Our Front Door"

This true story is dedicated to

My Dad, Thomas C. Gee,

My brothers,
Thomas E. Gee, Donald Chris Gee,
Robert N. Gee

And my Aunt, Barbara J Wilkinson —

With Much Love

Beverly J. Raffaele

See more photos at the end of the story.

This is a true story and every effort has been made to make it as accurate as possible. The story is told in my own words and then there are excerpts of the personal accounts of others that survived the tsunami and had to begin to rebuild their lives.

Beverly J. Raffaele

If you drive south on highway 101 to the nearest overlook, you will see the city wrapped around a perfect crescent shaped peninsula.

Beverly J. Raffaele

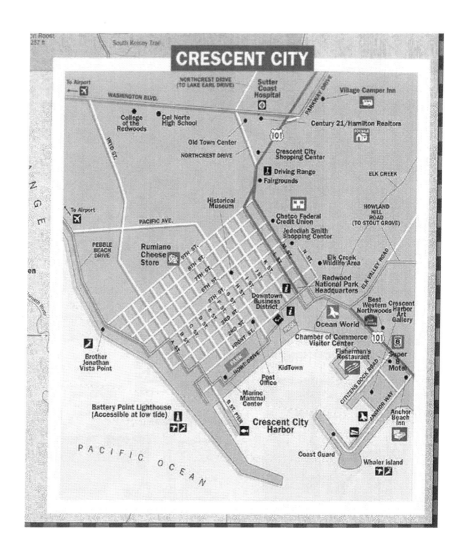

9

2 days after

Our house is the tall one to the bottom left of this aerial shot of Front Street. As children we would cross "Front Street" go through a sandy field and then down to the beach to play. We took a direct hit.

Texaco Tank Farm

Our Story

It was in the fall of 1960. Daddy was thirty years old when my mother left us for another man, leaving him to raise us four children alone.

Me, I was ten and a skinny little girl with round brown eyes and baby fine brown hair. I had three little blue-eyed blond brothers ages eight, six and five.

It was a worrisome time for Daddy. He was strong enough and loved his children enough to take the responsibility on.

I have great love and respect for my Dad. Three and a half years later, his strength was tested again.

March 27, 1964, dawned a crisp sunny day in Crescent City. Daddy had bought us new Easter clothes and he had the boys' outfits laid out on the couch. He had bought them new dress pants, shirts, shoes and socks. I picked out a pretty skirt and blouse outfit and I took them upstairs to my room.

My Aunt Barbara had arrived on Friday evening by Greyhound bus from San Francisco to spend Easter with us. She had to go back on Sunday because she had to be back at work

Monday morning. That evening, when it was time for bed, she told Daddy that she would sleep downstairs on the couch. He insisted that she go upstairs and take my brother Tommy's bed. Daddy told her that Tommy could sleep with him.

It was a beautiful moonlit night and the ocean, in gun-metal gray, glistened with the light of the moon.

I was sleeping soundly when suddenly there was a large blast, so powerful that it threw me out of bed and onto the cold linoleum floor. I got up and ran to my bedroom window. The sky was on fire, and water was slapping against the house just inches beneath my windowsill! I ran in a panic into the boys' room where my Aunt Barbara had been awakened and shaken from the blast. Running back into my bedroom, I once again looked out my window. I wasn't sure if I was in a realistic nightmare or truly awake. What I saw made me think that I was sick and delirious: my Dad's 1955 cream-colored Chevrolet floated by.

Aunt Barbara came to my side. I could hear my little brothers yelling something through my haze and then the next thing that floated by was our landlord's Jeep; then I felt that and other things bump against the house.

Aunt Barbara was very calm and with that soft southern accent of hers, she simply said, "Beverly, it's a tidal wave."

She was former Marine stationed in Hawaii. She knew all about these things.

With those words, I suddenly realized that this was no dream and as I stared out the window in shock, I realized too that my Dad's bedroom was just beneath mine and the water was above the top of his window!

"Daddy!" I screamed in sheer terror. I ran from my room, through my brother's room and then I bolted for the stairs. Aunt Barbara grabbed me around the waist, but I broke free of her. Still screaming for Daddy and in a panic to get to him, I started to run down the stairwell. I was halfway down when I heard a horrible excruciatingly loud creak and then I felt the old house start to lean. At that moment, I thought that it was going to break away from the old Darby Building that the house was partially connected to, and then collapse over; but it was the main staircase breaking away from the wall.

I ran back to the top of the stairs, but then I remembered that my little brother Tommy had slept with Daddy to make room for Aunt Barbara. He was downstairs too!

"Daddy! Tommy!" I shrieked. The sounds and the smells were as if I was standing at the shore during a pounding squall but there was something else, I could smell gas.

The ocean roared, the big three-story house groaned against its power, I could hear wood splintering and large bangs as logs and debris came right through the front of our house.

My aunt kept an eye on me continuously; telling me to stay put while she was trying to keep my middle brother Donny from running down the stairs after me. He was running around like a wild little squirrel.

I stayed glued to the top of that dark stairwell screaming "Daddy! Tommy!"Over and over.

As the power of the wave receded, the tall old house leaned, making a horrible creaking sound and then after what seemed like an eternity, I heard a voice, say, "stay upstairs!" It was Daddy.

"Where's Tommy!" I yelled, trying to swallow the lump that was rapidly growing in my throat; then to my great relief, I could hear him crying and saying, "Daddy don't leave me, don't leave me." Then I heard Daddy say, "I won't Son, hang on."

I stood at the top of the stairs as Daddy and Tommy climbed toward me. I could barely see their forms in the damp darkness of the stairwell. I learned later that the wave hit around two o'clock in the morning. They reached me shivering, with their teeth chattering.

Daddy and Tommy's Experience Battling the Wave

I sat down with my dad at his kitchen table in October of 2005. I set down the tape recorder and then I asked Daddy to tell me what happened. He started slow at first but then as he talked, he started remembering names and details. This is what he told me.

"I had been awakened by the blast. I rose up to look out the bedroom window and saw water above my bed. The water rose to above the window and then I heard a roar. I jumped and stood up on the bed and then the water crashed through the front of the house and rushed into my room.

"The mattress began to fill up with water and then it began to fold up all around me and Tommy. The water started rising rapidly. I thought if the house was going to go, then I could try to get out through the window. I held Tommy up with one hand while I tried to pound the window with a piece of mushy driftwood. It wouldn't do anything so I started to frantically pound with my fist. I couldn't get anywhere with those small windowpanes and I ended up cutting a deep gash in my hand. I knew it was futile so now I had to find a way to keep Tommy and me from drowning. My hand was bleeding badly.

"Tommy started clinging to me as the water continued to rise. The mattress, being sponge rubber, began to float. Tommy was dragging me down so I shoved him up on the mattress. Now I was being swirled around and I was trying hard to tread water while fighting the debris that swirled around my legs. The water felt like ice! It was still rising and I kicked upward and then Tommy grabbed me around the neck and clung on like a monkey. He was pulling me down again so I told him, 'turn loose, you are going to drown us,' then I pushed him toward the ceiling for air. I had just under a foot of air left when we were suddenly drawn back and slammed against the bedroom wall. The outer wall of the room buckled in but my heavy iron bed held it. The wave was receding and the old house groaned in its wake.

"We had survived and we hadn't swallowed any ocean water which would have made us really sick. It was dark, all the lights were out, I could hear the Texaco gas tanks as they exploded and there was a strong smell of propane.

"I felt that it was time to try to get out of there and try to get upstairs. I knew it was a tidal wave and I didn't know what else was coming. Tommy held me tightly around the neck. I made him get down and he held tight onto my hand. I had to climb over something that was jammed in the doorway from the hall to the living room. I wanted to leave Tommy where he was for a minute because I didn't know if the stairs were there or not and I couldn't see well enough to know how dangerous it was. Tommy would not stay; he clung to me; so we felt our way through, climbing over piles of debris. I was cold, terribly cold."

When we met

Daddy's voice was shaking and he kept saying, "Stay up there, stay put."

"This way Daddy, this way," I said, as they made their way up the pitch-black stairwell. When they reached the top of the stairs, I ran and got a blanket and wrapped it around Tommy's trembling body. They were so cold! Daddy wrapped himself up in a blanket too. He didn't know what was going to meet us if we tried to get out of the house. The smell of propane was in the air and the flames from the fuel tanks that had exploded were flickering through the upstairs windows. So, we huddled on the beds, filled with fear and shock until daylight.

When daylight came, Daddy was able to find some old clothes that were in wooden bins built into the walk-through closet between the boys' big bedroom and my little one. He found two pairs of jeans with holes in the behind. One pair had a hole on one side and one had a hole on the other, so he put both of them on. He found an old blue sequined shirt, an old pair of shoes, and a coat.

From the living room of the house there were six steps and then a landing; it turned and then there was the stairwell that led to the second floor. The landing had given way and we made our way out by climbing down the stairs and over debris piled up against it. The front door had been busted open and the living room windows were broken out.

In the living room were logs, deep sand and junk. There was junk everywhere and amongst that junk was our living room furniture. The big wood heater that normally sat at the back of the living room was jammed solid in the doorway that led back to Daddy's bedroom. That was what Daddy and Tommy had to climb over to get out.

We heard voices and our landlord, Richard Childs, and another man were walking toward the front of our house where we were making our way out. Richard looked at Daddy with great relief and said, "I thought you had drowned."

We, as family, have held a grudge against Richard Childs. Daddy hates to make waves and he refused the press when they came in to see and photograph the house. He didn't want to be interviewed. To tell the real story, he would have to talk about his anger and he wasn't the type. You see, Richard Childs worked for the power company in Crescent City. His family had been pioneers in the little lumber town of Crescent City, California, and the three-story house that we lived in had been Richard's childhood home. The Childs were well known throughout the county. His wife Jacquie worked in city finance.

By ten o'clock that night, Richard had been radioed that there was a tidal wave coming. If he would have warned us, we would have went to higher ground or we would have gone into the Darby building that our house was connected to. There was a door in our house leading into it at the top of the first flight of stairs. The Darby building had two-foot thick brick walls. You couldn't hear it storm in there. It was a hundred years old and had withstood tidal waves, cyclones, and earthquakes.

Instead of warning us, in all fairness, I am just guessing this, Richard Childs, being raised on that block, had seen many tsunamis over the years but none that had devastated all of Front Street. Anyway, he was standing out on the sidewalk when one wave crossed Front Street, came up to the curb and then receded. What he didn't know was, as that wave receded, it nearly emptied out the harbor and a twenty-one foot wave was right behind it. He said that when he was radioed that the big one was just offshore, he barely had time to run in the house to get his wife and dog and escape up the alley between our houses, to Second Street, then to Third Street and so on. He said that all the while the water was nearly on his bumper.

The next morning when he returned, the house that he and his wife lived in just across the alley from ours was split in two and one end had floated around and met the other.

When we made it outside and saw their little ranch style house destroyed, we thought they had been killed. When Daddy saw him coming up the alley, he was as relieved to see Richard, as Richard was to see us.

Richard offered us rooms in the Dodge Inn. It faced Second Street and had sustained little damage.

"Take as many rooms as you need and stay as long as you like, Tom," he told my dad.

Jacquie Childs fed us all breakfast and then Daddy told us to go to bed and get some rest. I didn't want to go to bed – I was curious and I wanted to hear everything and see everything. I obeyed Daddy but for just a little while.

We went up a wide stairway carpeted in thick floral carpeting. The banisters were heavy dark wood and the hotel was furnished with antiques. Once in the room, with its old hand carved dresser and beveled mirror, I headed for the steel framed double bed. The sheets were cold, white and starchy. They felt horrible on my legs so I crawled between the blanket and the bedspread and curled up to try and rest, but my eyes were wide open.

Daddy, in the meantime, was taking inventory. He didn't have a car; our 1955 Chevy was across the street perched up on a city sand pile. The 1956 Chevy Wagon that he had overhauled was still in the garage, but it was filled with whatever the ocean brings in and the water had naturally got up into the wiring, so it was no good.

Then I got up and went back to the house with Daddy and we left the boys at the Dodge Inn with Aunt Barbara.

Daddy and I climbed around in the house to see what all was lost. In the kitchen, there was a tire up on our kitchen counter along with many other foreign objects that included oil cans and other debris. Much to Daddy's relief, our old white china cupboard and sideboard had floated on its back like a boat. On the top shelf of that old cupboard, he kept our family photos in a little red overnight case that Daddy has to this day. He also had our birth certificates, titles to the cars and other important papers on that shelf. They were all dry.

The most important thing to him though, was finding his wallet. There was six hundred dollars cash in it. He muscled away the jammed wood heater from the doorway that led back to his room and we went in to search for it. The room didn't have a closet, but it had a big antique armoire in it. It had been toppled over by the wave and it was laying on its front. When Daddy had gone to bed the night before, he had pulled off his slacks and laid them in the floor beside the armoire. We lifted and pushed to move the armoire over and there laid Daddy's slacks with his wallet still in the back pocket.

We had our lives, our upstairs bedroom furniture, six hundred dollars in the bank and the six hundred dollars in Daddy's wet wallet. He also had a month's wages coming from Peterson Brothers lumber mill where he worked.

Even though that was all we had to our name, we felt blessed just to be alive.

Later that day, Daddy had a friend of his take him to look for a car. He paid one hundred dollars for an old 1956 Plymouth to use for work. Then he went back in to find all the clothes that he could salvage. He pulled them out of the old armoire and he pulled more out of the debris and sand. Then he went uptown to the Laundromat to wash them. The man that owned the Laundromat didn't like it because he didn't want the sand getting in the motors of his washing machines. But he allowed Daddy to use them. He had to wash everything twice. He cleaned the washing machines out and then ran them through again. The owner helped him although he hated to see him coming with another load.

The Red Cross set up a station in the community center up town. It was the perfect place for an intake station because it was so large and it had not been reached by the wave.

Daddy wanted to talk to them about housing. I was in an office filling out papers for us and Daddy was out in the foyer talking to folks, including someone from the local radio station. The list of the dead was going to be broadcast. I don't know if he said, "My daughter isn't with me and her name is Beverly" or what, but the broadcast said, "Thomas Gee, and sons, Thomas, Donald and Robert are accounted for, but daughter Beverly is missing."

I still don't know how it happened, but my mother who was living in San Francisco at the time, heard the broadcast and became hysterical. As soon as highway 101 was cleared, Aunt Barbara left by Greyhound bus to go back to San Francisco because she had to work and Mom came in. She went directly to our house on Front Street and when she saw the devastation, she became physically ill.

Back at the community center, a man by the name of Bud Hendricks said that he had a house for rent and he told a worker at the Red Cross that he would let us have it for the first month free. After the paperwork was filled out, a man from the Red Cross went with Daddy to look at our house. He was shocked at the destruction of the downstairs. He carefully climbed upstairs with Daddy and saw that we had our twin beds, our clothes and dressers. The Red Cross, God bless them, gave us vouchers to buy furniture for the living room, kitchen and one bedroom. We needed household goods, groceries, and the things it takes to supply a home: dishes, pots and pans, towels and more. They gave us one hundred thirty-five dollars for small essentials. That amount of money went a long way in 1964.

Bless his heart, was Bud Hendricks ever glad to see Daddy. When he approached him, they shook hands and he said, "Tom, I thought you had drowned."

We had the vouchers, but there wasn't any new furniture in town. The furniture store had been flooded out and we couldn't go to Eureka, Grants Pass, or even to Brookings to buy anything because we had no way to haul it.

Crescent City had a second hand store and auction house. We got the best second hand furniture they had. It wasn't great but it was clean and usable. We also needed a washer and dryer. Our old dryer was sitting up on the attic stairs of the woodshed and our washing machine had salt water in the motor and debris inside the tub. We used the Laundromat until those could be replaced.

The police department gave those that lived in the tidal wave zone tags to wear so that they could come and go without being stopped because there was looting going on. The jewelry store, two banks, oil from the Shell and Texaco stations, liquor bottles from the liquor store, clothes from the clothing store, merchandise from Safeway and so much more, was scattered everywhere and the looters swarmed on it.

The National Guard came in and they sealed the area off. Daddy couldn't get downtown to get his money out of the bank and although the bank was flooded, the money was secure so it wasn't a loss. Now, after losing everything, it was time for him to set up housekeeping again. He did just that too and I am so very thankful that my father is a man of strength and character. I love and respect him very much. He had his job as a lumber grader for Peterson Brothers, and although he had to take time off for us to recover, they didn't dock him one penny. It was as if he hadn't missed the days that it took for him to get settled again. The lists of blessings are long and so are the lists of tragedy. We knew nearly everyone that had perished.

↓Our block was here Front St.

The Crescent City Harbor Now

Two days After

2 days after

Our house is the tall one to the bottom left of this aerial shot of Front Street. As children we would cross "Front Street" go through a sandy field and then down to the beach to play. We took a direct hit.

Where is my Father now? He is a healthy seventy-seven years old. He and his wife Bea, walk two miles every day that the weather permits. They love to garden, fish and enjoy each other's company.

Daddy in 1966

My mother passed away on November 26, 2001 with her family at her bedside.

The Destruction

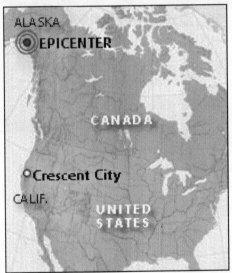

The following pages will give you accounts of others who survived the tidal wave of 1964. They are fascinating stories both tragic and compelling.

History

NPR.org Morning Edition, November 17, 2005

The Crescent City Harbor is one of the oldest in California. Lumbering and timber products are the major industries. Four waves struck the city. The travel time of the first tsunami wave to Crescent City was 4.1 hrs after the occurrence of the earthquake in Alaska. It caused no significant damage other than flooding.

On Good Friday in 1964, the largest earthquake ever recorded in North America struck Anchorage, Alaska. Shifting tectonic plates displaced billions of tons of ocean water and sent tsunami waves rushing at the speed of a jetliner down the coast of the Pacific Northwest. The tsunami struck several coastal communities on that March 27, but its biggest punch was saved for Crescent City, Calif., a small lumber and fishing town of about 3,000 residents just south of the Oregon border. It came by the light of a full moon in a series, it's believed, of four waves. The first wave caused only minor flooding of shops and stores in the small downtown area near the shore. But Crescent City residents were familiar with high water. They had also had their share of tsunami false alarms. So residents and shop owners weren't terribly distressed by the foot of water that flooded the lower blocks of downtown.

Photo courtesy U.S. Coast Guard

The Incredible Story of the Clawsons
and Clarence and Peggy Coon

A Report from Dateline NBC

Crescent City, not some ancient megalopolis swallowed by the sea, but a sleepy waterfront town on the northern edge of California. Forty years ago it was struck by a killer tsunami. It was March 27, 1964, at 5:36 p.m. A 9.2 magnitude earthquake shook the seafloor under Valdez, Ak, triggering a tsunami that went hurtling down the West coast.

Gary Clawson: "We just happened to be in the wrong place, the very worst place."

Gary Clawson, then 27 years old, owned a waterfront tavern in Crescent City, on around midnight after the initial wave hit and passed, he rushed to shore to check on his property. Along came both his parents and his fiancée.

Clawson: "It just seemed like that it was over with."

Mack McGuire: "You don't forget something like that."

After hearing the monster wave had receded, Mack McGuire also headed to the shore, to check on his fishing boat. He couldn't find it, so he too stopped by the waterfront tavern, where he and the Clawson gang all marveled at the damage, assuming the worse had come and gone.

But they were about to learn one of the most important lessons in handling a tsunami. Contrary to what you would often imagine, the first wave may not be the deadly one.

Suddenly a second wave hit.

McGuire: "Yes, very much surprised. I never had a wave like that hit me."

Clawson: "All of a sudden, I heard just kind of heard a rumble. And the whole west wall of that tavern just disappeared. It just crushed it in. Then all of a sudden the building itself, the whole tavern, left its foundation."

All were trapped on the tavern's roof, now barely above water. These two, then younger men swam off. Mack Maguire returned home to his wife, after lending a spare rowboat to Gary Clawson, who rushed to rescue his stranded parents and fiancée. They climbed onto the boat. The water was calm. Again, they all assumed the worse was behind them.

Clawson: "I had never been through a tsunami. Had no idea that when the water went down, it would go back out as fast as it come in."

They had almost reached dry land, when the tsunami's huge force sucked them back toward the ocean. The water was pulling them violently at speeds upwards of 300 mph, toward a small underpass under the flooded highway. Within seconds, the boat crashed into the metal grate.

Gary's father, mother, fiancée, and 3 other people on board all died. He was the sole survivor.

Four waves struck crescent city that night. The largest was over 20 feet high. The tsunami washed away 29 city blocks and killed 11 people.

Today there are still constant reminders of the tsunami here. Yes, it can happen again. The next one may be far bigger.

Eleven people in all died in Crescent City that night in what became known as the worst tsunami in the history of America's lower 48 states.

Susan Andrews of member station KHSU in Arcata, Calif., assisted in the reporting of this story.

Lighthouse keeper Peggy Coon's account of the tidal wave

"The water withdrew as if someone had pulled the plug. It receded a distance of three-quarters of a mile from the shore. We were looking down, as though from a high mountain, into a black abyss. It was a mystic labyrinth of caves, canyons, basins, and pits, undreamed of in the wildest of fantasies.

"The basin was sucked dry. At Citizen's Dock, the large lumber barge was sucked down to the ocean bottom. In the distance, a black wall of water was rapidly building up, evidenced by a flash of white as the edge of the boiling and seething seawater reflected the moonlight. The Coast Guard cutter and small crafts, that had been riding the waves a safe two miles offshore, seemed to be riding high above the 'wall' of seawater.

"Then the mammoth wall of water came barreling towards us. It was a terrifying mass, stretching up from the ocean floor and looking much higher than the island. My husband Roxey shouted, 'Let's head for the tower!' but it was too late. 'Look out!' he yelled and we both ducked as the water struck, split and swirled over both sides of the island. It struck with such force and speed that we felt like we were being carried along with the ocean. It took several minutes before we realized that the island hadn't moved.

"The wave crashed onto the shore, picking up driftwood logs along the beach and roadway. It looked as though it would push them onto the pavement at the end of A Street. Instead, it shoved them around the bank and over the end of the outer breakwater, through Dutton's lumberyard. Big bundles of lumber were tossed around like matchsticks into the air, while others just floated gracefully away."

The ocean covered the outer breakwater as it rolled over Dutton Dock. The surges left the huge lumber barge resting on top of Citizen's Dock. Once attached to a dock, the Citizen's fish storage buildings were now dancing over the ocean. Moored fishing boats bobbed up and down, and one boat tore up Elk Creek as if it was motorized.

Peggy Coons continued staring outside: "When the tsunami assaulted the shore, it was like a violent explosion. A thunderous roar mingled with all the confusion. Everywhere we looked, buildings, cars, lumber, and boats shifted around like crazy. The whole beachfront moved, changing before our very eyes. By this time, the fire had spread to the Texaco bulk tanks. They started exploding one after another, lighting up the sky. It was spectacular!

"The tide turned, sucking everything back with it. Cars and buildings were now moving seaward again. The old covered bridge, from the Sause fish dock, that had floated high on the land, had come back to drop."

Eleven people in Crescent City were killed by the tsunami. Twenty-one boats were destroyed in the harbor, and ninety-one homes in town were damaged. The total cost of all the destruction was in excess of seven million dollars.

The lighthouse survived the ordeal intact, but the following year, the modern beacon that replaced the Fresnel lens in the tower was switched off, and a flashing light at the end of the nearby breakwater served as the harbor's navigational aid. On December 10, 1982, the light in the lighthouse tower was lit again, and the Battery Point

Lighthouse was listed as a private aid to navigation.

The tsunami waves covered the entire length of Front Street, and about thirty blocks of Crescent City were devastated. Lumber, automobiles, and other objects carried by the waves were responsible for a good portion of the damage to the buildings in the area. Fires started when the largest tsunami wave picked up a gasoline tank truck and slammed it against electrical wires. The fire spread quickly to the Texaco tank farm, which burned for three days. Final tsunami damage in Crescent City was estimated at $7,414,000. (1964 dollars).

Special to the Chronicle / Bryant Anderson

Law offices

Second Street

Beverly J. Raffaele

Texaco tank farm

California Tsunami Victims Recall 1964's Killer Waves

Willie Drye
National Geographic News

January 21, 2005

The news of the December 26 tsunami had special
resonance for residents of Crescent City, California. Their waterfront
town of about 7,500 was devastated when a tsunami swept in from the
Pacific Ocean early on March 28, 1964. The business district was leveled, and 11 people were killed.

Gary Clawson is still trying to make sense of what happened on that long-ago night. The ferocious waters spared him but killed his parents and his fiancé. The survivors of the Indian Ocean tsunami—which killed more than 225,000—will endure the same puzzled agonizing for the rest of their lives, he said.

"I've lived (the 1964 tsunami) two or three times a week since it happened," Clawson said from his current home in Florence, Oregon, just up the coast from Crescent City. "You can't define how it felt, or what you go through when you can't breathe. You have to live that experience to know what it's like."

Clawson said he would never understand why he didn't die. "It probably took me four or five seconds to go through (the tsunami), and it would take me 15 minutes just to tell you everything I thought of while it was happening," he said.

Alaska Cities Devastated

On the afternoon of March 27, 1964, Alaska was shaken by an earthquake even stronger than the recent Indian Ocean quake. Anchorage and other Alaska cities were devastated, and more than a hundred people died. *Life* magazine reported that the quake unleashed "more than 2,000 times the power of the mightiest nuclear bomb ever detonated and 400 times the total of all nuclear bombs ever exploded."

From its center beneath Prince William Sound, the quake sent a tsunami rippling across the Pacific and down the coasts of Canada and the United States. Crescent City was a sitting duck for these waves, said

Dennis Powers, author of *The Raging Sea,* a book about the 1964 Crescent City tsunami that will be released January 27.

Powers said underwater topography can steer a tsunami toward a particular point along a coast and sometimes increase its power by concentrating its force. Crescent City sits on that kind of shoreline, he said.

"If Crescent City was at a different angle to the ocean, they wouldn't have had that destruction," Powers said. "Crescent City was a magnet for the tsunami."

Bill Parker, who was director of the town's civil defense department in 1964, said officials had been warned that earthquake-generated waves were headed their way. Such warnings were nothing new. Crescent City had had "a lot of watches and evacuations" for tsunamis, Parker said. "They didn't develop into anything," he said.

Still, Parker and others spread the warning. Soon after midnight, the first wave reached Crescent City. It was small and had little effect. But the worst was yet to come.

Clawson was in his family's bar celebrating his father's 54th birthday with his parents, his fiancé, and a few friends when a 21-foot (6.4-meter) wave swept into the harbor. "We were in the tavern when the wall of water came in," he recalled. "It took the building away, probably went back 100 yards [about 100 meters] or so."

Sucked Into a Culvert

Clawson managed to get to a rowboat and get survivors into it. But when the deadly wave receded, it sucked the occupants into a large culvert. Somehow, Clawson survived, but his parents and fiancé didn't.

Dawn's light revealed stupefying destruction. Crescent City's business district was gone, and fuel tanks near the harbor were afire. Automobiles, debris, and the ruins of buildings were piled in seaweed-covered heaps. "When daylight came, we were just dumbfounded," Parker said. "We couldn't believe what we were seeing.

Crescent City is the only town in the continental United States where people have been killed by a tsunami. Reminders of the tragedy are abundant in the town, and residents take tsunami warnings very seriously.

Tom Sokowloski, a retired physicist who worked at federal tsunami warning centers in Alaska and Hawaii, said coastal residents everywhere would be wise to follow Crescent City's example, because it could happen again.

"It behooves you to learn how to protect yourself," Sokowloski said. "No warning center can help you if you're right next to the source (of the tsunami)."

The only way to escape a tsunami is to head to higher ground the moment you hear the warning, Sokowloski said.

And the threat of a tsunami isn't limited to the Pacific coast. Some scientists are concerned that a region of instability beneath the Caribbean Sea could cause a deadly tsunami along the East Coast from Miami to Washington, D.C.

There's also the possibility that the eruption of an obscure volcano in the Canary Islands off the coast of Africa could send giant tsunami waves surging ashore from New York to Florida, as well as southern Britain.

A slab of rock about 35 miles (56 kilometers) long on the western slope of the volcano

Cumbre Vieja is cracking. Scientists think an eruption could shear the slab away from the mountain, drop it into the sea, and send gigantic waves rolling across the Atlantic Ocean. About nine hours later, these waves—some of them 80 feet (24 meters) high—could strike the U.S. East Coast.

The volcano's most recent eruptions were in 1949 and 1971. Some scientists say the next eruption could cause the cataclysmic tsunami, while others say such an event isn't likely for hundreds of years, if at all.

Sokolowski thinks coastal residents everywhere need to be clearly warned of the dangers of tsunamis. And the warnings need to be systematic and continual to make sure new residents are aware of the danger, he said.

"One of the most effective things in a tsunami warning system is the education of the public to do what they have to do," he said. "It's really important for experts to come in again and again and to go into the schools. Otherwise, the danger is forgotten."

Willie Drye is the author of Storm of the Century: The Labor Day Hurricane of 1935, *published by National Geographic Books.*

Don't Miss a Discovery
<u>*Sign up our free newsletter.*</u> *Every two weeks we'll send you our top news by e-mail (<u>see sample</u>).*

ACKNOWLEDGEMENTS

"The Raging Sea" by Dennis Powers available online at Amazon.com and other online bookstores. Or visit his website at http://www.dennispowersbooks.com/author.html

REFERENCES

COX, D.C. and Pararas-Carayannis, George. A Catalog of Tsunamis in Alaska. World Data Center A – Tsunami Report, No. 2, 1969.
GRANTZ, A.G., G. Plafker, and R. Kachadoorlan, 1964.
Alaska's Good Friday Earthquake, March 27, 1964: A Preliminary Geologic Evaluation, U.S. Geol. Survey Circ. 491, 35 pp.
KACHADOORIAN, R., 1965.
Effects of the Earthquake of March 27, 1964 at Whittler, Alaska, U.S. Geol Survey Prof. Paper 542-B, 21 pp.

KACHADOORIAN, R. and G. Plafker, 1966.
Effects of the Earthquake of March 27, 1964 at
Kodiak and Other Communities on the Kodiak
Islands, U.S. Geol. Survey Prof. Paper 542-F, 41
pp.
LEMKE, R.W., 1966.
Effects of the Earthquake of March 27, 1964 at
Seward, Alaska, U.S. Geol. Survey Prof. Paper
542-E, 43 pp.
PARARAS-CARAYANNIS, G., 1965.
Source Mechanism Study of the Alaska
Earthquake and Tsunami of 27 March 1964: Part
I. Water Waves, Univ. of Hawaii, Hawaii Inst.
Geophys. Tech. Rpt., HIG 65-17, pp. 1-28
PARARAS-CARAYANNIS, G., 1967.
Source Mechanism Study of the Alaska
Earthquake and Tsunami of 27 March 1964, The
Water Waves. Pacific Science. Vol. XXI, No. 3,
July 1967.PARARAS-CARAYANNIS, G.1972.
"A Study of the Source Mechanism of the Alaska
Earthquake and Tsunami of March 27, 1964."
Volume on Seismology and Geodesy on the Great
Alaska Earthquake of 1964, National Academy of
Sciences, Washington D.C., pp 249- 258, 1972.
PLAEKER, G. and R. Kachadoorian, 1966.
Geologic Effects of the March 1964 Earthquake
and Associated Seismic Sea Wave on Kodiak and
Nearby Islands, Alaska, U.S. Geol. Survey Prof.
Paper 543-D, 46 pp.
PLAFKER, G. and L.R. Mayo, 1965.
Tectonic Deformation, Subaqueous Slides and
Destructive Waves Associated with Alaskan March

27, 1964 Earthquake: An Interim Geologic
Evaluation, U.S. Geol. Survey, Menlo Park, Calif.,
21 pp
SEISMOL. DIVISION, USC & GS, 1964.
Preliminary Report: Prince William Sound,
Alaskan Earthquake, March-April 1964, U.S. Coast
and Geod. Survey, 83 pp.
WOOD, F., ed., 1966.
The Prince William Sound, Alaska, Earthquake of
1964 and Aftershocks, v. 1, Operational Phases,
U.S. Coast and Geodetic Survey, No. 10-3, 263

Made in the USA
Lexington, KY
12 September 2010